I dedicate this book to the Ancestral souls who crossed over
— S. W.

For Grandad, Jeanette, and Elvis
— J. D.

Atheneum Books for Young Readers
An imprint of Simon & Schuster Children's Publishing Division
1230 Avenue of the Americas
New York, New York 10020

Book design by Ann Bobco and Sonia Chaghatzbanian

The text of this book is set in Bembo.
The illustrations are rendered in watercolor.

Printed in Hong Kong

2   4   6   8   10   9   7   5   3   1

Library of Congress Cataloging-in-Publication Data
Williams, Sheron.
Imani's Music / by Sheron Williams ; illustrated by Jude Daly—1st ed.
p.   cm.
Summary: Imani, an African grasshopper, brings music to the new world when he travels aboard a slave ship.
ISBN 0-689-82254-5
[1. Grasshoppers—Fiction. 2. Slavery—Fiction. 3. Music—Fiction. 4. Storytelling—Fiction.] I. Daly, Jude, ill. II. Title.
PZ7.W6668175 Im 2000
[E]—dc21   98-019119

FIRST
EDITION

IMANI'S music

by sheron williams   illustrated by jude daly

Atheneum Books for Young Readers
New York London Toronto Sydney Singapore

BORN DURING THE PLANTING SEASON of eighteen nine and aught, my grandfather W. D. was
a man of the "Used-to-Be" who resided in the "Here-and-Now" 'cause time and living life had
dragged him there. He was hailed in five counties as a storyteller that could wrestle a tale
to the ground. He danced on the path 'tween the "Used-to-Be," the "Here-and-Now," and the

"What's-Gon'-Come." Shoot, it was folks like him that fed the path and kept it alive.

W. D. had an old walking cane that he carried with him everywhere he went. Claimed it was crafted from the discarded planks of the slave ship that brung his daddy's daddy over. He said as long as he owned that cane, no slave ship could own no piece of him.

Every so often, he'd circle the house
dragging that cane in the dust behind him,
carving a faint line on the ground. Then he beckoned
us to him with a knobby hand, and we'd all come running,
'cause inside that circle, W. D. could step over the river of time
like it was a rain-puddle pond. With his first few words
and a faint sprinklin' of night air, we'd all be there
together, in the land of Used-to-Be, like it
was the Here-and-Now.

That's 'cause folks is folks, and things don't change that much from time to time. Everybody still looking to be loved. Folks still getting married and trying to raise children. Hunger still drives folks to find food. And laying folks to eternal rest still prompts close kin to cry.

"Be careful," he'd say as we drew close to listen. "Don't get your feet wet in the river of time; step lightly over into the land of Used-to-Be."

Used to be a time when there was no music on the planet. Music was such a delectable dish that the Ancestors kept it to themselves and had a taste each and every day. It was set high on a shelf in the night sky in gigantic, shiny, black bowls. From time to time a puffy wind or rainstorm would jostle those bowls, causing a bit of music to fall to the earth. But the world never knew what it was missing. That's 'cause nearly every creature that could take cover did, 'cept for one faith-filled, music-loving soul called Imani.

Unlike other grasshoppers Imani loved to have the rain fall on him. He found, during each rainstorm, he'd been given a wonderful gift. He was able to rub his hind legs together on a leaf or blade of grass and make the most beautiful sounds. Something that good you don't want to keep to yourself, and as he joyously played a palm frond or a potato vine, he found himself wishing the rest of the world could share his gift.

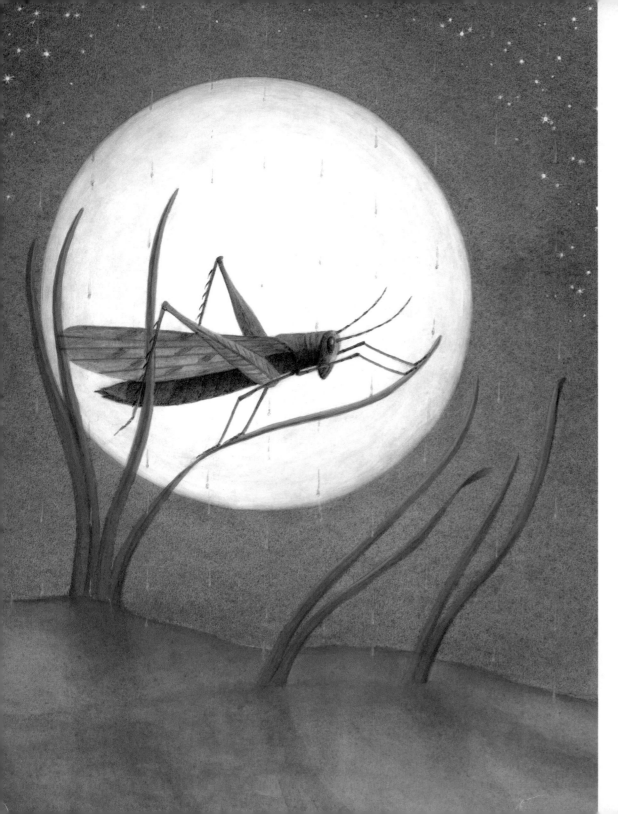

So, one special evening when a soft rain fell, Imani chose a regal blade of Serengeti grass to play, bowed low, and dedicated his performance to the Ancestors. He played and played to the black sky. He played with a special prayer held deep inside. As the last lilting note of his song escaped into the night air, he whispered with all the faith he could muster, "Please, Ancestors, give music to the world."

Now when the Ancesters looked down from where they were and heard the first few bars of Imani's beautiful song, they saw how happy it made him. "That's one song-making grasshopper," they agreed. "We'd certainly consider giving him music on a permanent basis." Laughing and dancing so hard they rocked Heaven and Earth, they poured their music out of all the black bowls. A wallop of tune fell on Imani, and the world soaked up the rest like a sponge.

Now music was everywhere and in everything. The gift of music fell on all of Imani's grasshopper kin, though they were only able to play their legs, not the petals and grasses.

It fell on lions and giraffes; it fell on snakes and birds (a lot fell on birds 'cause they were flying when it fell). It fell on trees and mountains and cacti and people! If you don't believe it, just you thump or jiggle or gently prod anything on earth, and listen to its music leak out.

At first people added their voices to Imani's songs. Then musicians created instruments to play along with him, coaxing out the music stored in reeds, trees, animal skins, ivory, copper, and bronze, creating flutes, drums, banjos, guitars, xylophones, lyres, and harps.

Soon everything was done to music. Farmers harvested their crops to it. Kings were serenaded as they took long and thoughtful walks. Laborers felled trees and built villages to worksongs. Lovers sang love songs. Merchants sang out the virtues of their wares. And kingdoms heralded the passing of power from generation to generation with royal instruments and song.

Imani searched everywhere
for new greenery to play. He
traveled over mountain ranges
by day and sang his songs on the
grasslands by night. Farmers and
merchants and herdsmen,
charmed by his songs, gave him
guidance and direction.

One day, a well-traveled
cloth merchant named Umoja
pointed west and said to him,
"The tallest grasses grow near
the shore, grasshopper. Go and
sing them! The oceans echo
their sounds. Sing them sweet!
The waves will carry your song
across the oceans. Sing on!
Travel with me, grasshopper,
I will guide you."

Imani did just that, and they became fast friends. Umoja wove cloth by profession and with love he wove an excellent flute song. Their voices blended well and their campfire never lacked for company.

Then, on a bright and blinding morning Imani and Umoja reached the coast. There at its edge were huge boats singing, *"Cush, cush, cush."* The voice of the sand sang under their feet, *"Grish, grish, grish,"* and the waves went, *"Lap, lap, lap"* against the shore. Added to their song

were voices speaking strange tongues and the sound of metal chains, *"Clink, clink, clink."*

"What strong music these elements play together," Imani exclaimed. "I must add my voice." But, exhausted from his journey, he decided to nap. He nestled into Umoja's sack of threads and cloth.

Imani was shaken awake by the sad cries of people, the *clink, clink* song of the metal chains, the *roosh, roosh* song of the moving ocean, and the shouts of Umoja, who was caught in a net of many strings. Somehow, some way they had gotten themselves on one of those boats. And, Ancestors help them, the boat had set sail!

Horrified, Imani began to cry. He was leaving his homeland, his friends, his family, and his beloved Serengeti grass! The ocean was all around them! It played strange and sad music, accompanied by clinks of metal, rooshing waves, and the voices of people. Drying his tears, Imani reached for the comfort of his music and bravely sang all night.

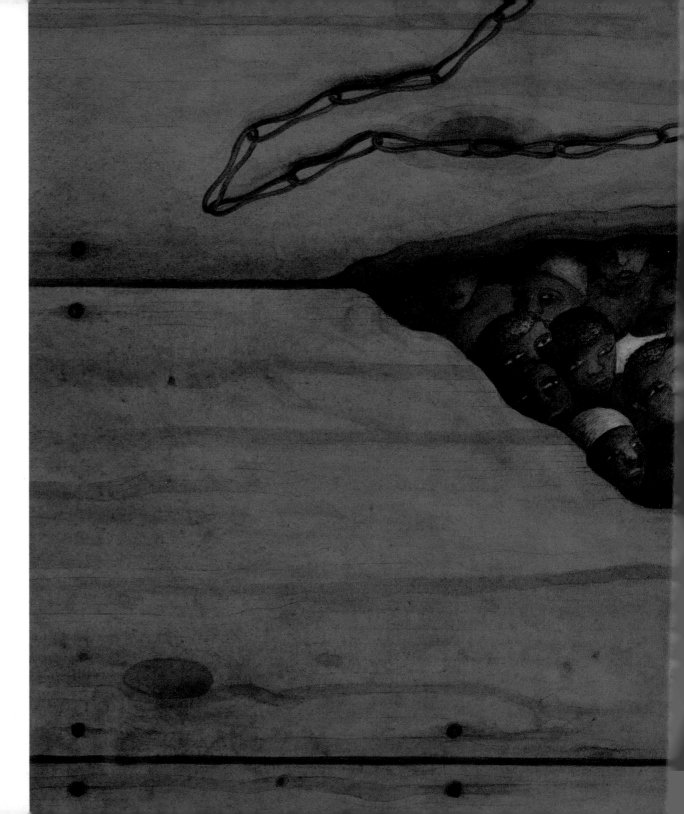

Through a tiny opening on the deck's floor, Imani could see a multitude of humanity, packed together one on top of another, hundreds of men, women, and children linked by a common chain. They were the merchants, the farmers, and the herdsmen he had met on his journeys, and they cried out to him in KiSwahali, Yoruba, and many other languages.

"Grasshopper, bring us water, we thirst!"

"Grasshopper, bring us food!"

And many begged him, "Grasshopper, tell my mother where I have gone and that if I can return to her, I will."

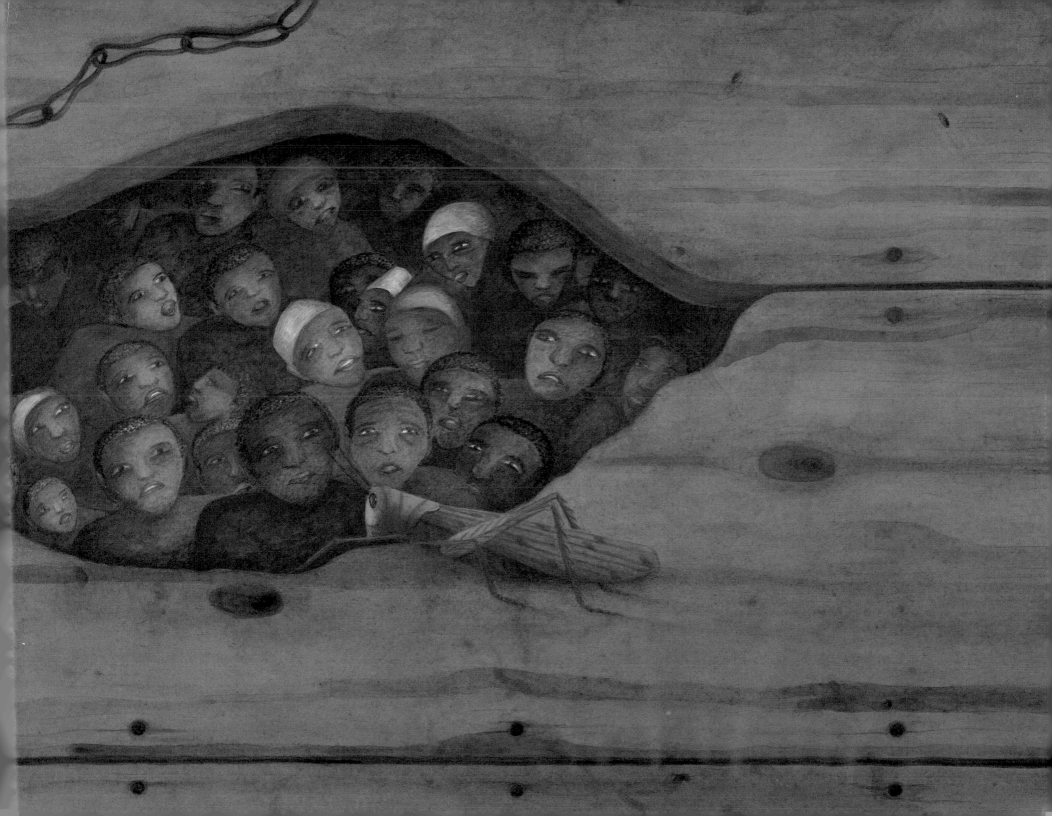

To hear and see what lay below the decks took the song right out of Imani. How could he do what they asked? Imani's own mother did not know where he was. In that moment Imani knew that his people's fate would be his fate, and his tears began anew.

"Do not cry," a voice said from beneath the deck. "Your tears cannot help us." Imani's spirit brightened, for he knew that voice—it was Umoja. "To fetch water and food for so many cannot be done by you, little one. Busy yourself with what you can do. Give us music! Give us hope!"

"Yes!" said Imani. "They will need music wherever they are going; it may be all they have."

From ship's stores to ship's galley, from captains' quarters to crow's nest, Imani sang every grain and bit of vegetation he could find on that boat. He learned new songs. He sang them bittersweet, but he sang on!

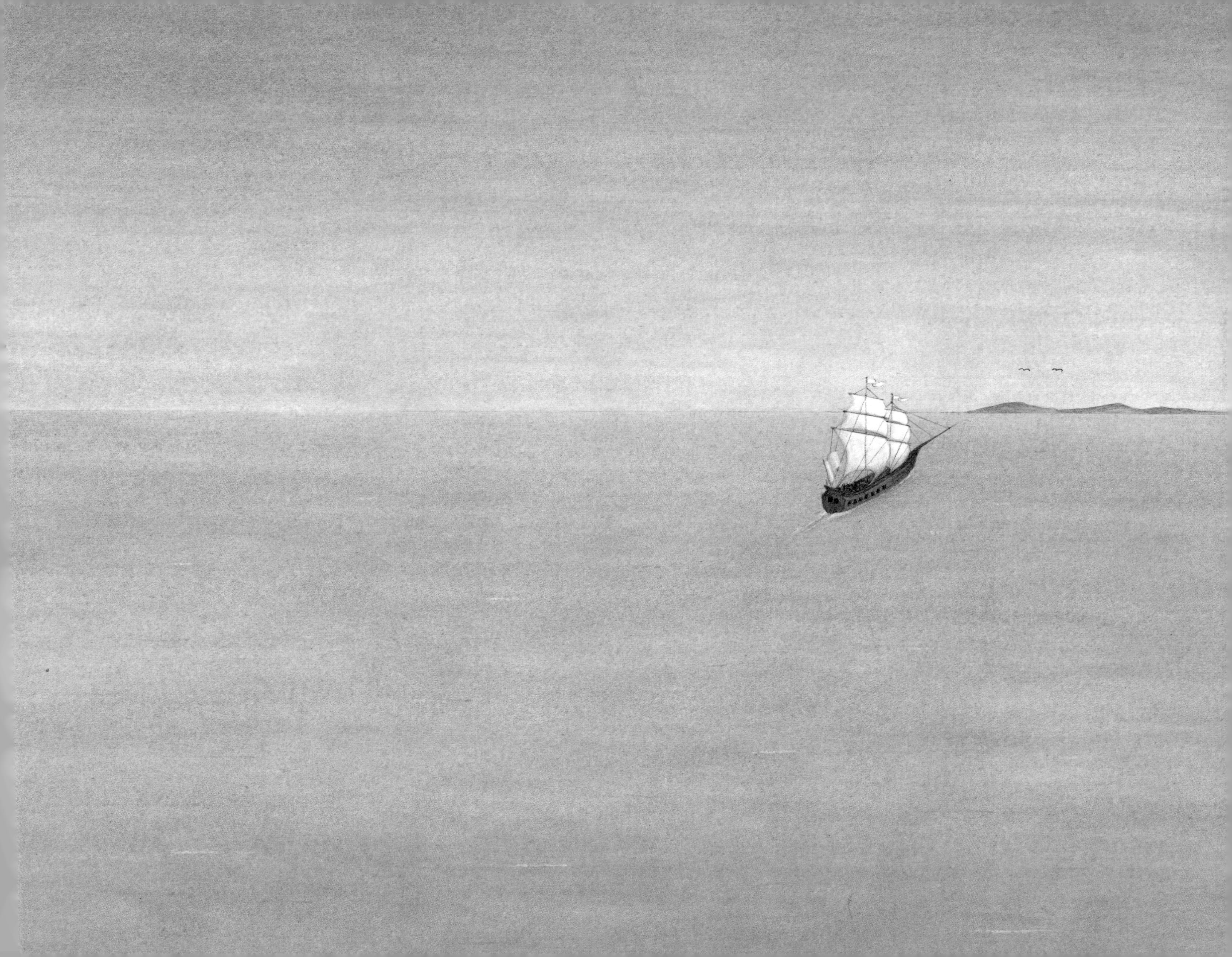

When the boat finally ceased its rocking and landed on a new shore, Umoja and the others were led away in many directions. Imani was alone. He searched and searched but there was no African millet, no sorghum, no bulrushes from the Nile. Lost to him forever was the lilting music that leaked out of a single blade of Serengeti grass. He called to the farmers and herdsmen and merchants he happened upon for guidance and direction, as he'd always done, but they didn't understand him.

Imani roamed the new land. He didn't leave one cornhusk untwanged or polk green untweaked in his search for new sounds that would tickle an Ancestor and bring hope to his people. He never found Umoja, but when he happened upon one or two of the hundreds who had come over with them, he taught them his new songs. They taught these songs to others.

"Where there was once Yoruba and others," he told them, "now there is one people, one language, one music. In this new land you must live, love, work, and comfort one another, bound together by new songs." And so it was they learned these new songs. Sometimes they sang them bittersweet, but always they sang on!

During his travels Imani met a lady grasshopper named Hope. She translated his name into her own tongue and called him Faith. Faith married Hope and they had many, many children. Imani passed on to them the ability to sing.

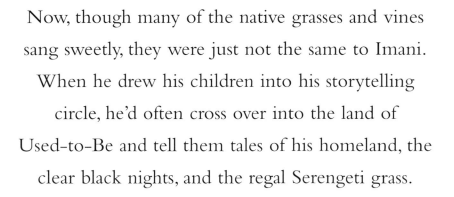

Now, though many of the native grasses and vines
sang sweetly, they were just not the same to Imani.
When he drew his children into his storytelling
circle, he'd often cross over into the land of
Used-to-Be and tell them tales of his homeland, the
clear black nights, and the regal Serengeti grass.

As Imani and Hope grew old, their children's children took up his search for new songs to
sing. They still can be heard today in the Here-and-Now, searching among the grasses and vines
for a lilting sound that can rock Heaven and Earth and tickle an Ancestor.

On a clear black night, if you listen carefully anywhere you go, you can hear Imani's children's children as they sing their songs.

Do they not sing well for grasshoppers whose grandfather sang in a strange tongue in a strange land?

Also by Sheron Williams

And in the Beginning

illustrated by Robert Roth